DELAWARE BRANCH
ALBANY PUBLIC LIBRARY

D1105164

Down by the Station

Down by the Station

by Jennifer Riggs Vetter

Illustrations by Frank Remkiewicz

TRICYCLE PRESS

Berkeley

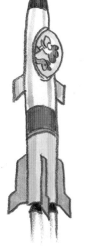

Listen to the tune at www.tricyclepress.com

Text copyright © 2009 by Jennifer Riggs Vetter
Illustrations copyright © 2009 by Frank Remkiewicz

All rights reserved. Published in the United States by Tricycle Press, an imprint of the Crown Publishing Group, a division of Random House, Inc., New York.
www.crownpublishing.com
www.tricyclepress.com

Tricycle Press and the Tricycle Press colophon are registered trademarks of Random House, Inc.

Design by Betsy Stromberg
Typeset in Beton
The illustrations in this book were rendered in watercolors.

Library of Congress Cataloging-in-Publication Data

Vetter, Jennifer Riggs, 1968–
  Down by the station / by Jennifer Riggs Vetter ; illustrations by Frank Remkiewicz.
    p. cm.
  Summary: This illustrated version of the traditional song expands and describes more vehicles, different locations, and their unique sounds, from puffer-billies to race cars and rockets.
  1. Children's songs, English—United States—Texts. [1. Songs. 2. Vehicles—Songs and music.] I. Remkiewicz, Frank, ill. II. Title.
   PZ8.3.V712664Do 2009
   782.42—dc22
   [E]
                                                    2008011308

ISBN 978-1-58246-243-1
Printed in China

11 10 9 8

First Edition

For Paul, Kurtis, and Milo

—J.R.V.

For Austin, Anthony, Alex, Jack, and Zack

—F.R.

Down by the station, early in the morning
See the little puffer-billies all in a row
See the engine driver pull the little lever

Puff puff toot toot! Off we go!

Down by the depot, early in the morning
See the yellow school buses all in a row
See the school bus driver warming up the engine

Vroom vroom
beep beep! Off we go!

Down by the truck stop, early in the morning
See the mighty tractor trailers all in a row
See the friendly trucker pulling on the air horn

Pull pull waHONK! Off we go!

Down by the work site, early in the morning
See the giant excavators all in a row
See the operator digging with the bucket

Clank clank scrape scrape!

Off we go!

Down by the airport, early in the morning
See the jumbo jet planes all in a row
See the airline pilot push the throttle forward

Roar roar whoosh whoosh! Off we go!

Down by the water, early in the morning
See the bobbing sailboats all in a row
See the salty skipper pulling up the mainsail

Flap flap splash splash!

Off we go!

Down by the racetrack, early in the morning
See the speedy race cars all in a row
See the fearless driver revving up the engine

Rrrm rrrm zoom zoom! Off we go!

Down by the firehouse, early in the morning
See the shiny fire engines all in a row
See the firefighter turning on the siren

Weeooo weeooo! Off we go!

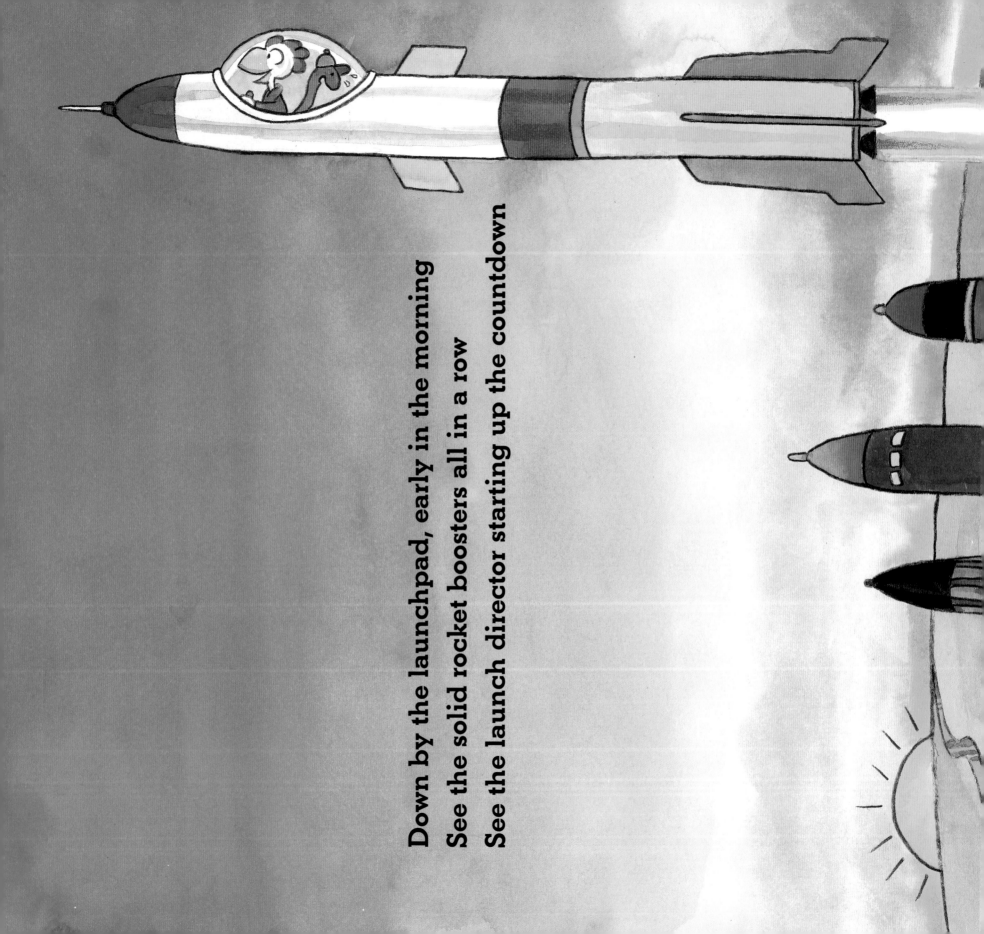

Down by the launchpad, early in the morning
See the solid rocket boosters all in a row
See the launch director starting up the countdown

Down by the station, later in the evening
Everybody's sleepy at the end of the day
See the engine driver stop the locomotive

Shhhhhhh...

Here we stay!